Farshore

First published in Great Britain 2021 by Farshore

An imprint of HarperCollins*Publishers*
1 London Bridge Street, London SE1 9GF
www.farshore.co.uk

HarperCollins*Publishers*
1st Floor, Watermarque Building, Ringsend Road
Dublin 4, Ireland

Written by Chloe Pearce
Designed by Jeannette OToole

© 2021 Disney Enterprises, Inc.

ISBN 978 0 7555 0105 2
Printed in Italy
001

A CIP catalogue record for this title is available from the British Library.

Parental guidance is advised for all craft and colouring activities.
Always ask an adult to help when using glue, paint and scissors.
Wear protective clothing and cover surfaces to avoid staining.

Stay safe online. Farshore is not responsible for content hosted by third parties.

Farshore takes its responsibility to the planet and its inhabitants very seriously.
We aim to use papers from well-managed forests run by responsible suppliers.

Disney
FROZEN
ANNUAL 2022

belongs to ....
....

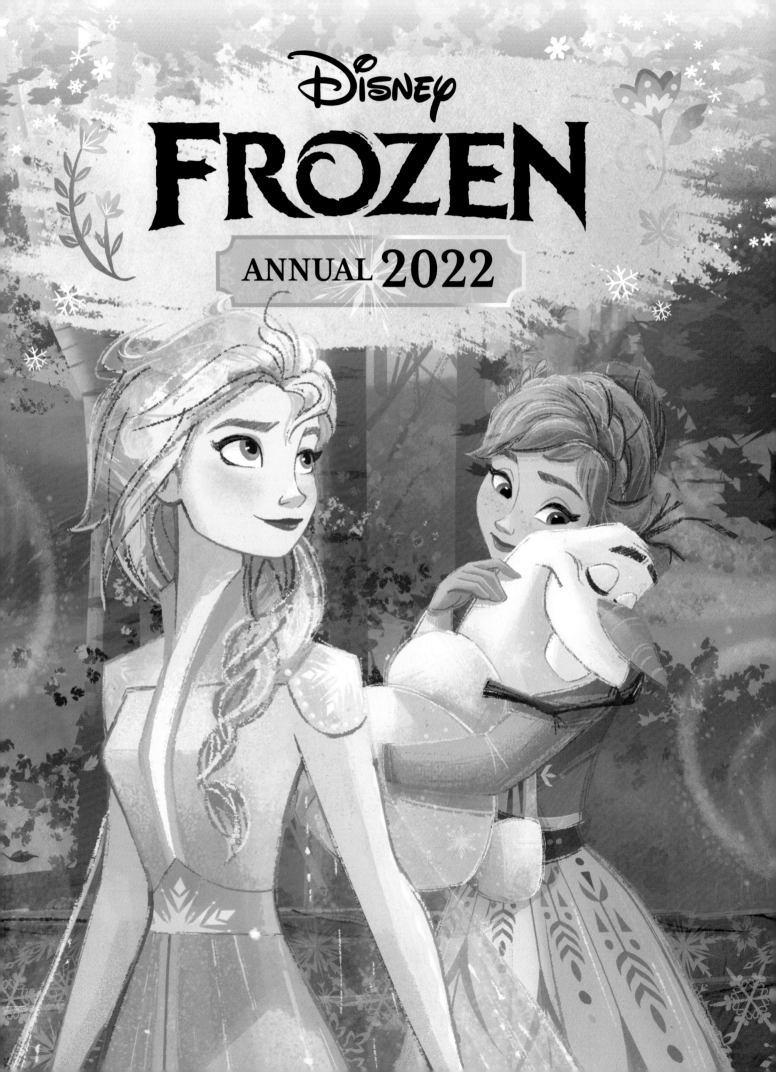

Contents

Closer than Ever

Anna, Elsa and their group of friends have grown, and their bond is stronger than ever. Join them on their journey into the unknown ...

Olaf is a cheerful snowman brought to life by Elsa'a powers. He loves nothing more than warm hugs and dreams of the wonders of summer.

Elsa was born with the power of ice and snow. She loves her family and kingdom but deep down, she longs to understand where her powers came from.

Anna would do anything for her friends and family. She is very brave and is always ready for the next adventure.

Sven is Kristoff's best friend and Kristoff can always count on his loyalty. He will do anything for his friends … or for a crunchy carrot!

Kristoff is an ice harvester brought up by trolls in the mountains. He has always preferred reindeers to people but has a soft spot for Anna.

Welcome to Arendelle

Arendelle is a beautiful kingdom set in the mountains. Elsa welcomes you to Arendelle Castle, a place full of secrets and surprises ...

Come and Explore

It's easy to get lost in the huge castle grounds. Match the letters in the picture to the castle parts listed below. Then, write the matching letter in each box. The first one has been done for you.

a

The Bell Tower — a

The Main Entrance — ☐

The Guard Tower — ☐

The Main Pinnacle — ☐

Answers on page 67

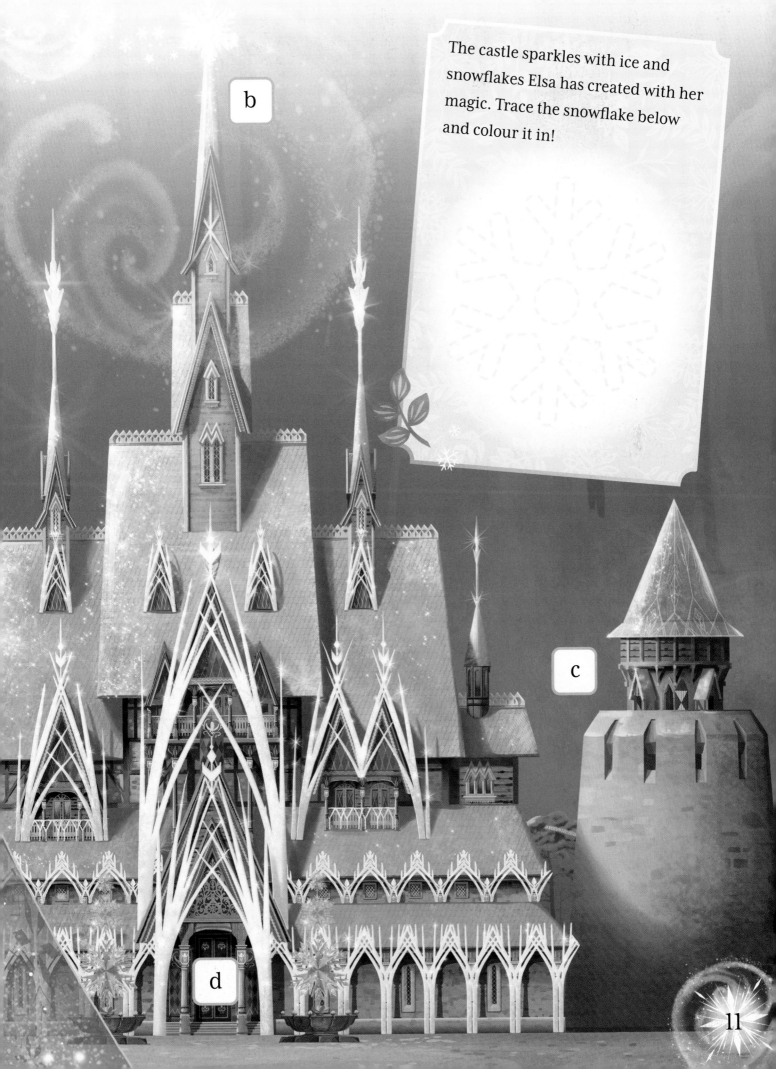

The castle sparkles with ice and snowflakes Elsa has created with her magic. Trace the snowflake below and colour it in!

b

c

d

Do You Want to Build a Snowman?

Help Anna and Elsa put Olaf together. Trace over the words to reveal what they will need.

snow

twigs

coal

carrot

Join the dots to finish putting Olaf together.

Snowball Battle

It's another snowy day in Arendelle, so Anna and Elsa are going to have a snowball fight! Join them and play this board game with a friend.

START

1 20
2 19
3 18
4 17
5 16
6 15
7 14
8 13
9 12
10 11
11 10

How to play

It's a game for 2 players.

· You'll need a dice and two counters.

· Each player chooses a character and places a counter at their respective starting positions. Take turns rolling the dice and moving the number of spaces shown.

· The aim of the game is to block your opponent's progress by sending them backwards.

· For example, if player A rolls 5 and advances, but after 3 spaces meets player B blocking the way, then player A must move back 2 spaces.

· The player who succeeds in sending their opponent back to the start wins.

16
5

15
6

17
4

14
7

18
3

13
8

19
2

12
9

20
1

START

A Special Shed

Script by: Tea Orsi; Layout: Sara Storino; Clean: Sara Storino; Color: MAAWillustration

ANNA AND KRISTOFF ARE PLANNING A SPECIAL DAY FOR THE VILLAGE KIDS...

SLED GAMES

SIGN UP HERE!

THE GAMES WILL TAKE PLACE NEXT SUNDAY AND WILL LAST FROM DAWN TILL DUSK.

OH, HILDA AND LARS WOULD LOVE TO TAKE PART IN THEM!

EXCELLENT, I'LL SIGN THEM UP!

?!

I'LL BE RIGHT BACK!

HI THERE! WOULD YOU LIKE TO SIGN UP FOR THE SLED GAMES?

?!

NO, THANKS!

HMM... THAT WAS ODD.

DO YOU KNOW THAT BOY?

HIS NAME'S ERIK.

HE NEVER SLEDS WITH US.

HE'LL PLAY OTHER GAMES—JUST NO SLEDDING.

WHY IS THAT?

WE DON'T KNOW.

HE JUST ALWAYS RUNS OFF BACK HOME WHEN WE BRING OUR SLEDS.

WHERE DO ERIK AND HIS FAMILY LIVE?

IN A SMALL HOUSE NEAR THE RIVER. WHY?

SLED GAMES

ERIK'S SHY ABOUT SLEDDING WITH THE OTHER KIDS. SO I'D LIKE TO SIGN HIM UP FOR THE SLED GAMES TO HELP HIM FEEL WELCOME TO JOIN IN THE FUN.

GOOD IDEA! GO AND SEE HIM TOMORROW!

GOOD MORNING, ERIK! ARE YOU BUILDING SOMETHING?

PRINCESS ANNA?!

OH, THERE HE IS! WHAT IS HE DOING?

SORRY, I DIDN'T MEAN TO STARTLE YOU! I'VE JUST COME TO ASK YOU IF YOU WANT TO TAKE PART IN THE SLED GAMES.

I CAN'T...

WHY? IT'LL BE SO MUCH FUN!

I KNOW. I WISH I COULD, BUT I... I DON'T HAVE A SLED!

MY MOM AND DAD ALWAYS WORK UNTIL LATE, AND CAN'T HELP ME BUILD ONE...

I'M SURE THEY WOULD LOVE TO HELP YOU IF THEY HAD TIME.

I'VE MADE SOME SKETCHES OF WHAT I'D LIKE.

19

WELCOME! ARE YOU READY TO BUILD YOUR SLED WITH US?

WE ARE ALL LOOKING FORWARD TO HELPING YOU!

WOULD YOU REALLY DO THAT FOR ME?

OF COURSE! WE REALLY WANT YOU TO TAKE PART IN OUR RACE!

LET'S GET STARTED NOW!

LATER...

OKAY, I THINK WE'RE DOING IT RIGHT!

OF COURSE WE ARE!

SEE? THE MORE YOU TIE THE REINS NEXT TO THE TOP OF THE SKI, THE QUICKER YOU WILL STEER.

THAT'S AMAZING! BUT...

DO YOU THINK WE CAN ADD THIS FIN? I THINK IT WOULD KEEP THE SLED STEADIER WHEN YOU PICK UP SPEED.

I'VE NEVER SEEN ANYTHING LIKE THAT, BUT IT SOUNDS LIKE A GREAT IDEA!

AND, AFTER TWO DAYS OF HARD TEAMWORK...

IT LOOKS EXACTLY LIKE THE SLED I HAD IN MIND!

THANK YOU, EVERYONE! YOU'VE MADE MY DREAM COME TRUE!

WE ARE HAPPY YOU ARE JOINING IN THE RACE, AND HELPING YOU WAS FUN.

YES, BUT NOW...

LET'S GO BREAK IT IN!

YESSS!

FINALLY, THE SLED GAMES CAN BEGIN!

HEY, MAYBE WE SHOULD UPGRADE OUR SLEDS, TOO! KRISTOFF, WILL YOU HELP US?

ERM...

HAHAHA!

The End

21

Ready to Ride

To build his sled, Erik needed the right tools and the help of his friends. Can you help Erik finish his sled?

Working Together

Rearrange the jumbled pieces to match the picture by writing the numbers in the blanks.

Essential Equipment

Join the matching pairs to find the tool Erik needs to build his extraordinary sled!

A must-have Tool

Here's the other essential tool Erik used. Tick ✔ the matching silhouette of his hammer!

Answers on page 67

Stronger Together

With help from your friends, anything is possible. Have fun colouring this picture.

Crack the Code

The names of some of your favourite Frozen characters are missing some of their letters. Can you fill in the missing letters in each of the names?

S V _ N
_ O _ A F
K R I _ T O F F
_ N N A

Now work out which name is revealed using the letters you've written:

....

Odd Sven Out

Kristoff and Sven are best friends who know everything about each other. Can you tell which of these pictures of Sven is the odd one out?

a

b

c

d

e

Answers on page 67

Best Friends

Best friends are always there for each other. Who is your best friend? A friend can be someone you go to school with, a family member or even a pet. Draw a picture of you and your best friend.

My best friend is …

The Winter Shop

Script: Tea Orsi; Layout: Alberto Zanon; Cleanup: Letizia Algeri; Colour: Stefania Santi

DURING A LOVELY HIKE IN THE SNOW...

LOOK! IT'S VIOLET AND VITA FROM THE **PLANT** SHOP!

WHY ARE THEY COLLECTING PINE CONES?

DO YOU NEED HELP?

OH, HELLO, YOUR MAJESTIES!

WE'RE GATHERING ALL WE NEED TO MAKE WINTER WREATHS...

OH, I SEE YOU WANT TO MAKE A **LOT** OF THEM!

YES! WE HAVE A PLAN!

AS YOU KNOW, WE USUALLY DON'T HAVE MANY CUSTOMERS IN THE COLD SEASON...

BUT THIS YEAR WE'LL TRY TO **INCREASE** OUR SALES!

WE'RE TURNING OUR SHOP INTO A **WINTER WREATH SHOP!**

WHAT A WONDERFUL IDEA!

YOU COULD ALSO MAKE **GARLAND** AND **PINECONE** ARRANGEMENTS. EVERYBODY LOVES THEM THIS TIME OF YEAR!

THOSE ARE GREAT IDEAS! WE'LL MAKE A VARIETY OF WINTER DECORATIONS.

WE'LL **HELP** YOU FIND MORE MATERIALS!

AT SUNSET, AFTER A HARD DAY'S WORK...

THANK YOU! WITH ALL OF THIS, WE'LL BE ABLE TO MAKE MORE THAN ENOUGH DECORATIONS.

WE LOOK FORWARD TO SEEING THEM ALL AT YOUR SHOP!

30

SWISH

31

I HOPE THIS WILL CATCH SOME ATTENTION!

HOW COULDN'T IT?!

LOOK! IT'S A FOUNTAIN MADE OF ICE!

IT'S BEAUTIFUL!

HEY, THE PLANT SHOP IS SELLING DECORATIONS!

WINTER SHOP

I DIDN'T EVEN KNOW IT WAS OPEN DURING WINTER.

HAVE YOU STARTED A NEW BUSINESS?

YES, I HOPE YOU LIKE IT, MRS. ADAMSEN.

The End

Make a Leaf Wreath

Here's how to make your very own wreath, just like Violet and Vita's. Hang your wreath on your bedroom door as the perfect way to greet your friends!

You will need:

Two lids (big and small)
Strong card
Pencil and scissors
Paintbrush
Paint
Liquid glue
Dry leaves (or make your own from paper)
Ribbon
Optional extra decorations

1 Use the lids to DRAW two circles on the card. One big and one smaller in the centre.

2 CUT around the larger circle, then CUT out the middle section, as shown.

3 PAINT the ring orange. Let it DRY, then loop a ribbon and tie it around the back. Attach dry leaves with liquid glue, slightly overlapping them.

4 You could decorate your wreath with extras like flowers, holly or pine cones. Your wreath is now ready to hang on your door!

ASK AN ADULT TO HELP YOU!

Winter Market

The Arendelle Market is in full swing. Can you help find all of the things on Anna's shopping list?

GLOVES
BOOTS
CAKES
FRUIT

E	K	Z	O	M	N	S	R
P	A	B	C	D	G	I	C
M	H	O	T	S	E	V	A
G	L	O	V	E	S	R	K
U	X	T	E	I	S	E	E
O	C	S	Z	A	W	F	S
Y	E	U	K	M	P	O	U
T	B	F	R	U	I	T	N

Answers on page 67

Troll Trouble

Kristoff was raised by the wise trolls in the mountains.
Can you spot the 5 differences between these pictures?

1

2

Answers on page 67

Journey To Troll Valley

Elsa and Anna know they can always rely on the trolls' wisdom whenever they need advice. Help them find the right path to the Troll Valley.

a   b   c

FINISH

Answers on page 67

New Friends

In Frozen 2, when Anna and Elsa enter the Enchanted Forest, they meet the Northuldra and the Arendelliane soldiers who have been trapped there. Let's get to know them!

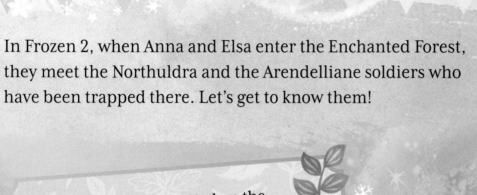

Beautiful leaves are carried on the wind in the Enchanted Forest. Add the missing leaves to complete the grid so that each type of leaf appears only once in each column and row.

a b c d

Answers on page 68

Mattias

When King Agnarr was a child, Lieutenant Mattias served as his official guard and was very fond of him.

Only one of these characters comes from Arendelle. Follow the paths to see who's connected to the crocus, the kingdom's symbol.

Ryder

He is a young Northuldran who wants to break the spell of the forest's mist and explore the great plains.

Honeymaren

She's a brave girl who will help Anna and Elsa discover more about their family's past.

Yelana

She's the leader of the Northuldra, loves listening to nature, and does her best to protect her people.

39

Misty Maze

The Enchanted Forest is surrounded by a thick magical mist. Can you help Elsa and her friends find their way through the mist and into the forest?

40

Answers on page 68

Forest Friendship

Honeymaren helps Anna and Elsa discover the truth about their parents and bring peace to the Enchanted Forest. Colour in this picture of Honeymaren.

DISNEY
FROZEN II

The villagers of Arendelle have been pushed out of the kingdom by the forces of nature. Does it have something to do with the haunting voice Elsa keeps hearing? Together with Anna, Olaf, Kristoff, and Sven, she decides to go to the Enchanted Forest to find out.

When they reach the Enchanted Forest, they discover that the Arendelliane soldiers and the Northuldra have been trapped there for many years because they angered the spirits of nature with their fighting. A Northuldran girl named Honeymaren tells Elsa about Ahtohallan, the river that contains the answers to the past. Elsa knows she must travel there to right the wrongs of the past.

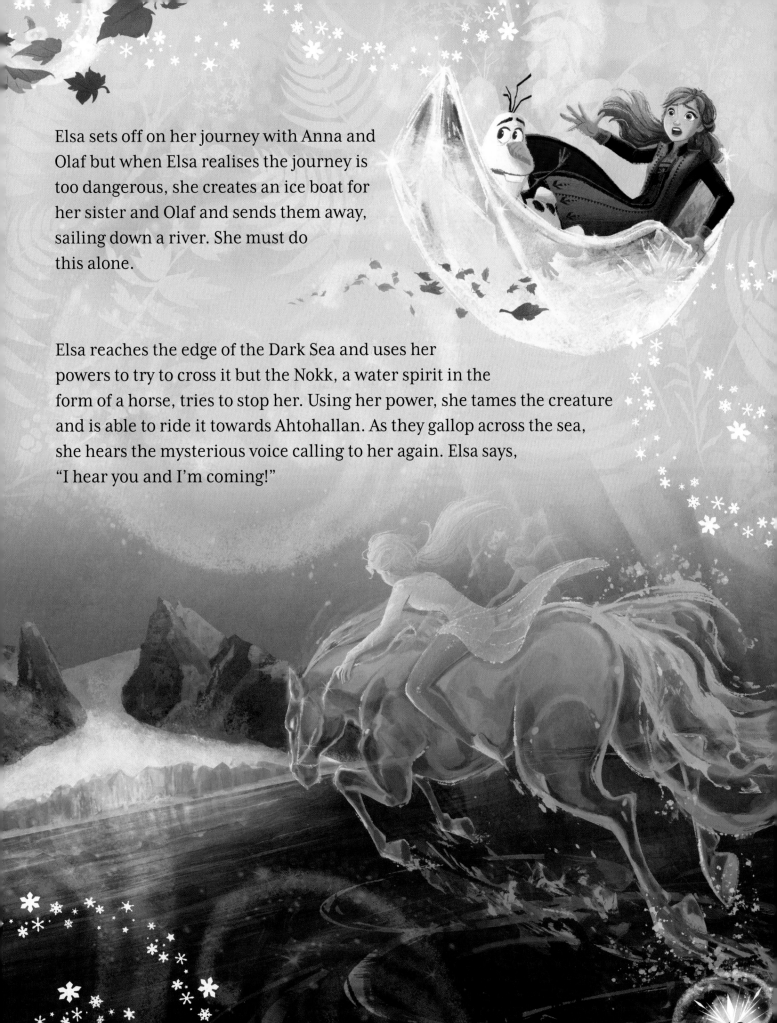

Elsa sets off on her journey with Anna and
Olaf but when Elsa realises the journey is
too dangerous, she creates an ice boat for
her sister and Olaf and sends them away,
sailing down a river. She must do
this alone.

Elsa reaches the edge of the Dark Sea and uses her
powers to try to cross it but the Nokk, a water spirit in the
form of a horse, tries to stop her. Using her power, she tames the creature
and is able to ride it towards Ahtohallan. As they gallop across the sea,
she hears the mysterious voice calling to her again. Elsa says,
"I hear you and I'm coming!"

When Elsa reaches Ahtohallan, she discovers it is a glacier – a frozen river of ice. She leaps from the Water Nokk and cautiously enters the dark ice cave. She can hear the voice calling from deep inside the icy caverns.

Eventually Elsa reaches a big open room where blurry images dance across the icy walls. They encourage her to show herself and grow into something new. That's when Elsa realises the mysterious voice is the memory of her mother, Queen Iduna, who is calling to her.

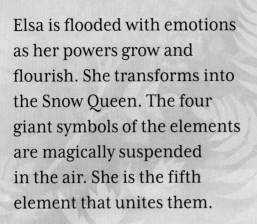

Elsa is flooded with emotions as her powers grow and flourish. She transforms into the Snow Queen. The four giant symbols of the elements are magically suspended in the air. She is the fifth element that unites them.

Elsa then begins to search through all the memories contained in the cave to try and find out what happened in the Enchanted Forest on the day of the battle between the Arendellians and the Northuldra.

When she finally finds out the truth about the lies that were told, the ice surrounds her, moving up her body and freezing her solid! With her last breath, she desperately sends Anna a message to share what she has learned.

The story continues on page 52.

45

A Blast of Magic

After following the voice that was calling to her, Elsa finds Ahtohallan and enters the magical ice cave. Help her use her ice magic to discover the truth.

Mysterious Figures

Strange images appear in the night sky. Tick ✔ the shapes that match the figures in this scene. Tip: There are two intruders!

Glimmering Ice Crystals

Match up the missing ice crystal dominoes to complete the sequence. TIP: BEWARE OF ONE INTRUDER.

Answers on page 68

The Elements

The spirits of the Enchanted Forest are magical creatures that represent each of the elements in nature. Match each description to the correct spirit element by drawing a line between them.

2

1

Earth Giants
This sleepy spirit hides in the rocky mountains. When woken, its strength can cause a quake.

Bruni
This cute little creature may be small, but his fiery spirit can cause great destruction.

Gale
This mischievous spirit likes to cook up a storm and sweep people off their feet.

Nokk
This powerful spirit guards the Dark Sea. Only with great skill can it be tamed.

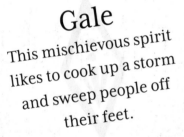

3

4

Answers on page 68

Colour in these pictures and bring the elemental spirits to life!

Which Sister are You?

Take this quiz to find out which sister you are most like.

When you meet someone new, you:

1 a. Chat with them and make instant friends

b. Can be a little shy around new people

At a party, you like to:

2 a. Dance, of course!

b. Get back home as quickly as possible

Can you keep a secret?

3 a. Not always!

b. Yes, secrets are always safe with me

What do you do if you have a problem?

4 a. Ask friends or family for advice

b. Keep it to myself

How would you like to celebrate your birthday?

5   a. Throw a huge party and invite everyone I know

     b. Meet up with a small group of close friends

What kind of holiday would you prefer?

6   a. Somewhere exciting with plenty of adventure

     b. Somewhere quiet where I can enjoy nature

What would you wear on a cold, wintery day?

7   a. Something warm and cosy

     b. Something elegant – the cold never bothered me anyway!

MOSTLY A
You are Anna
You're outgoing, positive and fun-loving but sometimes your adventurous spirit can get you into scrapes! Your family and friends mean everything to you.

MOSTLY B
You are Elsa
You are quiet and reserved and it may take you some time to open up to people. To those who know you well, you are thoughtful, caring and fiercely loyal.

DISNEY FROZEN II

Continued from page 42...

Meanwhile, in the Lost Caverns, Anna and Olaf are looking for a way out. Elsa's magical message reaches them, forming a memory out of ice. Now Anna knows the truth: Their grandfather built the dam to weaken the Northuldra's waters and lands. He caused the battle that trapped the Northuldra and Arendelliane soldiers in the Enchanted Forest. "We have to set things right! We have to break the dam!" Anna says.

Then flurries of snow start to float off Olaf's body. The magic is fading! Anna knows this means Elsa is in trouble. "Elsa's gone too far. I'm sorry, you're gonna have to do the next part on your own ..." Olaf says as Anna hugs him.

"I love you," Anna whispers as Olaf disappears.

52

Anna takes a deep breath and climbs out of the cave. She has to be strong and destroy the dam, even though the release of the waters will destroy Arendelle.

Anna soon finds the Earth Giants. She shouts as loud as she can: "Wake up! Come and get me! This way guys!" She begins to run, leading the giants towards the dam.

Meanwhile, Kristoff and Sven are searching the woods for Anna when they hear a loud noise and feel the ground shaking underneath them. The giants are chasing Anna!

"Throw your boulders!" Anna shouts to the giants. The Earth Giants lob huge boulders and the dam starts to crumble in front of her and is collapsing. Anna tries to jump from the structure but it's too far! Luckily, Kristoff grabs her just moments before she falls!

When the dam crumbles, the water races towards Arendelle. The people of Arendelle and the trolls watch in fear as a huge wave rushes towards them … but it's Elsa on the Water Nokk! Just as the waters are about to wash the kingdom away, the Snow Queen uses her powers to push the water away with an ice shield.

Thanks to Anna and Elsa's bravery, the fog clears and everyone in the Enchanted Forest looks up in amazement. The curse has been broken and they are finally free! The anger between the Arendelliane soldiers and the Northuldra disappears and they all celebrate their new lives as friends.

Anna and Elsa hug each other, reunited with tears of joy. Elsa explains to Anna that now she is the Snow Queen, she belongs with the elemental spirits, while Anna will become Queen of Arendelle.

Then Gale, the Wind Spirit, sweeps in carrying some snowflakes which Elsa uses to bring Olaf back to life. Olaf is very happy to be back and hugs everyone.

But the surprises are not over, as Kristoff suddenly kneels in front of Anna and holds out the ring he has been carrying in his pocket. "Anna, you're the most extraordinary person I've ever known and I love you with all I am. Will you marry me?" he asks. "Yes!" Anna says, bursting with joy.

56

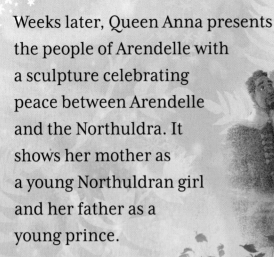

Weeks later, Queen Anna presents the people of Arendelle with a sculpture celebrating peace between Arendelle and the Northuldra. It shows her mother as a young Northuldran girl and her father as a young prince.

Just then, Gale appears, whirling around Anna. Anna holds up a note with a message for Elsa which Gale sweeps up out of the kingdom.

Gale takes the note to Elsa in the Enchanted Forest. The note says, "Charades Friday night. Don't be late. And don't worry, Arendelle is doing just fine. Keep looking after those spirits. I love you."

Even though they live apart, the sisters feel closer than ever, confident that together they will keep peace and balance in the world.

The End

Frozen Quiz

Put your Frozen knowledge to the test in this quick-fire quiz!

1

What is the name of Elsa and Anna's kingdom?

a. Ahtohallan

b. Arendelle

c. The North Mountain

2

What is the name of Kristoff's reindeer friend?

a. Ben

b. Sven

c. Ken

3

What is Olaf?

a. A snow angel

b. A snow monster

c. A snowman

4

Who is the leader of the trolls?

a. Grand Pabbie

b. Grand Pebble

c. Grand Pablo

5

What is Kristoff's job?

a. Ice harvester

b. Fisherman

c. Baker

6

Who is the leader of the Northuldra?

a. Yelana

b. Mattias

c. Ryder

7

What is the Wind Spirit called?

a. Breeze

b. Gale

c. Hurricane

8

What kind of creature helps Elsa get across the Dark Sea?

a. Dolphin

b. Turtle

c. Horse

9

Whose is the voice that calls to Elsa?

a. King Agnaar

b. Queen Iduna

c. Anna

10

What does Anna have to do to free the Enchanted Forest?

a. Break the dam

b. Build a wall

c. Drain the river

How did you do?

8-10
EXCELLENT!
Wow, you're a Frozen super-fan – there's not much you don't know about the world of Anna and Elsa.

4-7
GREAT!
You know your stuff – watch the movies again and you'll soon be a super-fan.

0-3
KEEP TRYING!
That's ok – you just need to watch the movies a few more times!

Answers on page 68

Queen Anna

Now that Arendelle is finally safe, the kingdom is ready to celebrate Anna as the new queen!

Can you find each of the characters in the picture? Tick ✔ each character when you find them.

The sisters' bond is strong, as it has always been. Today Anna has an important message for Elsa. Find the thread that leads to her.

a b c

Answers on page 68

The Greatest Bond

Anna and Elsa have their differences, but they have a bond that can never be broken. Colour in this picture of the two sisters.

New Beginnings

Show Yourself

BELIEVE

in Yourself

6

Answers

A MUST-HAVE TOOL

- [ ]
- [ ]
- [✓]
- [ ]

Page 10
Welcome To Arendelle

COME AND EXPLORE

The Bell Tower	a
The Main Pinnacle	b
The Guard Tower	c
The Main Entrance	d

Page 25
Crack the Code

SV<u>E</u>N, OL<u>A</u>F, KRI<u>S</u>TOFF, <u>A</u>NNA

The missing name is ELSA

Page 22
Ready to Ride

WORKING TOGETHER

2
5
1
4
3

Page 26
Odd Sven Out

d - is the odd one out

Page 35
Winter Market

E	K	Z	O	M	N	S	R
P	A	B	C	D	G	I	C
M	H	O	T	S	E	V	A
G	L	O	V	E	S	R	K
U	X	T	E	I	S	E	E
O	C	S	Z	A	W	F	S
Y	E	U	K	M	P	O	U
T	B	F	R	U	I	T	N

ESSENTIAL EQUIPMENT

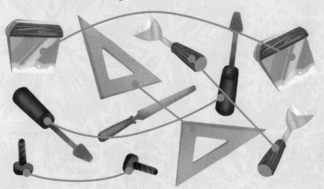

Page 36
Troll Trouble

More Answers

Page 37
Journey to Troll Valley
Path c leads to Troll Valley

Page 38
New Friends

Page 40
Misty Maze

Page 46
A Blast of Magic
MYSTERIOUS FIGURES

GLIMMERING ICE CRYSTALS

Page 48
The Elements
1. Bruni, 2. Nokk, 3. Earth Giants, 4. Gale.

Page 58
Frozen Quiz
1 - b, 2 - b, 3 - c, 4 - a, 5 - a, 6 - a, 7 - b,
8 - c, 9 - b, 10 - a.

Page 60
Queen Anna

Path b leads to Elsa.

Goodbye!